Crazy Crocs

Contents

Rhyming Moe
and the talent show

Moe just couldn't stand still. She couldn't
help it! At last, at last it was time to go. Time
to go to the talent show! Moe waddled up and
down, up and down, left to right, then right to
left, she was so excited.

"Moe, will you please stand still," Moe's
mum said crossly. "You're making me giddy."

"You're making my head spin," said Moe's
brother, Maxwell.

"I could make up a song about that ..." Moe began.

"NO!" Moe's mum and dad and brother said all together. "Please Moe, no!"
But Moe didn't hear them. Her mind started to tick and click with all kinds of rhymes.

"My head is spinning and giddy and dizzy,
And whirling and twirling and all in a tizzy!"
began Moe.

"Moe, I hope you're not going to make up any of your silly rhymes whilst we're watching the talent show," sniffed Maxwell.

"Hold on, Maxwell," said Moe, "I haven't finished my rhyme yet. I've fifty more verses to go yet!"

"Moe dear, you'll have to save them," said Moe's mum quickly. "If we listen to all of them now, we'll miss the first act."

"And the second, third, fourth and fifth," Maxwell muttered.

Moe didn't mind. Her rhyme could wait! This was her very first talent show and she was going to enjoy every moment of it. The talent show was held once a year, when all the animals came together and performed for each other. It wasn't a contest with prizes for the best and the second best act. It was more a chance for each animal to show the other animals what he or she could do.

"Let's get going then, or we won't get good seats," said Moe's dad.

4

And off they swam. Up through the murky, misty water of the watering hole and towards the bank.

They got very good seats. Right at the front of the crowd. It was even better than Moe thought. All the animals had gathered around the watering hole where the show was to take place. The late afternoon sun shone bright, bright, brightly and the air was alive with the sounds of all the different animals. Lions roared and turaco birds called, "Go away! Go away! Go away!" (although they didn't mean it!) and gorillas thumped their chests and snakes hissed happily and the hyenas laughed — even though the show hadn't even started yet!

A strong, stately lion came and stood before the huge crowd.

"Ladies and gentlemen," growled the lion in his deep voice. "Ladies and gentlemen. We start tonight's show with the monkeys – because they insisted on going first!"

Everyone laughed as the lion strode off, to
stand just beside Moe.
"Where are the monkeys?" asked Moe, looking
around. "I don't see them."
"Look up there, Moe. In the baobab trees,"
said Moe's brother.

Moe looked up and WOW! Five monkeys were swinging through the trees above her. They turned somersaults in the air as they dived from branch to branch, chattering cheerfully to the crowd below them.

"Oooh!!"

"Aaahh!!"

The crowd loved it! More than once, Moe thought that the monkeys were going to miss a branch and fall to the ground, but they never did.

"Do they have to show off quite so much?"
Moe's dad mumbled.

"Shush, dear!" said Moe's mum.

"The monkeys swing from tree to tree,
And how I wish that it was me!" Moe sighed.

"Oh dear!! She's off!" said Maxwell, her
brother.

At last the monkeys finished their display
and bowed to the audience who cheered and
whistled and roared their delight.

"I like the monkeys best," said Moe.

She decided right there and then that when
she grew up, she would be an acrobat and
swing through the trees just like the
monkeys. Moe turned her head to look at her
short, short legs and her long, long body.
Hhmm! Maybe she would be an acrobat on
the ground instead! Or better still, she could
be an acrobat in the water. After all, she could
spin round and round in the water,
faster than fast.

The lion strode out into the clearing beneath the trees. He announced the next act.

"Ladies and gentlemen, now we have the elephants," said the lion.

"Those of you with delicate hearing should stand well back." And the lion walked back to the crowd, to take his place next to Moe.

Four elephants walked out to stand before the crowd. A hush fell. Every animal was silent. One of the smaller elephants moved to stand before the other three.

"Hhhm!" said the lead elephant, clearing her throat. She raised her trunk, waited for a moment and then, "BRRRRAAAPPP! BRRRRAAAPPP!!"

The elephants began to trumpet out their music with the lead elephant conducting them with her trunk.

It was wonderful! Loud and so happy that you couldn't help sitting up straighter and tapping your paws or flapping your wings in time to the music.

"What a din!" whispered Moe's dad.

"Shush, dear," said Moe's mum.

As Moe listened, she thought it was the most wonderful music she'd ever heard.

"Now I know, without a doubt,
I want a trunk and not a snout!" said Moe eagerly.

"You'd look very strange with an elephant's trunk at the end of your face," said Maxwell. They all listened to the elephant band until they stopped playing.

"I like the elephants the best," Moe decided. And she was determined that when she grew up she would join the elephant band and play all kinds of rumpety-trumpety music. BRRRRAAAPPP!!

After the elephant band, there was a cheetah race. Three cheetahs had to race from the watering hole to a palm tree in the distance, where the ripe nuts could just be seen amongst the large green leaves.

"Ready ..." growled the lion. "Steady ... Go!"
And off they raced. The cheetahs moved so
quickly that soon they were nothing but a
blur.

"Why do the cheetahs have to run
everywhere?" grumbled Moe's dad. "If they
walked they'd still get to where they wanted
to be!"

"Shush, dear," said Moe's mum.

"Wow!" said Moe. "When I grow up I want to
be a cheetah!"

Maxwell creased up laughing. "Moe, when
you grow up you'll be a grown-up crocodile,
not a cheetah!"

"I like cheetahs, not crocodiles! I want to run and run for miles," said Moe crossly.

" You can always practise swimming until you can swim practically as fast as the cheetahs can run," said Moe's mum.

"All right. I'll do that instead," said Moe, cheering up.

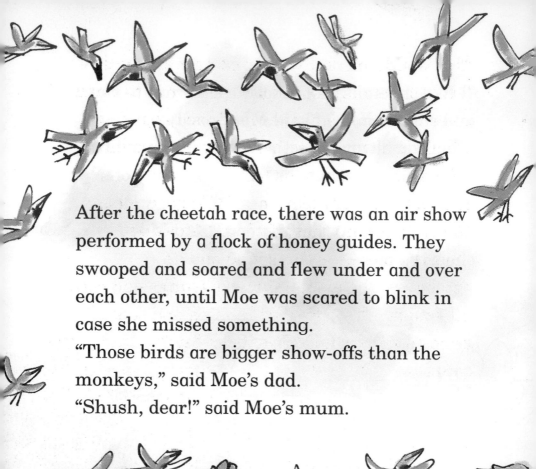

After the cheetah race, there was an air show performed by a flock of honey guides. They swooped and soared and flew under and over each other, until Moe was scared to blink in case she missed something.

"Those birds are bigger show-offs than the monkeys," said Moe's dad.

"Shush, dear!" said Moe's mum.

Moe wondered and wondered how it would
feel to have nothing around you but air. When
she walked her paws touched the ground and
when she swam there was water all around.
"Mum! Dad! I want to fly!
Let me! Let me! Please can I?" begged Moe.
"Moe, crocodiles don't fly," said Moe's dad.
"But the monkeys can swing and do
acrobatics, the elephants have trunks and can
play music, the cheetahs can run and the
honey guides can fly. What can I do?"
said Moe.

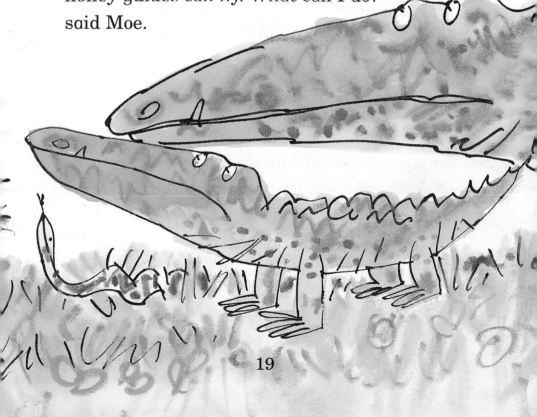

"What can you do?!" The lion who had been standing beside Moe spoke up. "My dear, I hope you don't mind, but I've been listening to your rhymes whilst the other acts were going on. I've never heard another animal rhyme as well as you."

"You wouldn't like it as much if you had to listen to it all day," mumbled Maxwell.

"Moe, how would you like to introduce the last act — the hippos?" asked the lion.

Moe's eyes grew wider than wide.

"Me!" she said. "Me! Introduce the hippos to all the other animals?"

"Yes. Why not?" smiled the lion. "With one of your rhymes."

"A short one," said Maxwell quickly.

"Okay!" Moe squeaked.

Moe walked out into the clearing with the lion, her tail shivering, her knees quivering, her whole body quaking. The lion cleared his throat. "Ladies and gentlemen, and now, to introduce the final act tonight, I present Rhyming Moe!"

Moe cleared her throat, then cleared it again.
She took a deep breath.
"I have had a splendid day,
There's not much more that I can say,
Except, before you go away,
It's time to let the hippos play!
To all of you – both far and near,
Let's end this evening with a cheer.
No fights, no fuss, no frowns, no fear,
And see you all, same time next year!"
The cheer that started after Moe had finished
her poem was deafening. Moe waddled back
to her family, as pleased as pleased.
"You were the best act tonight," smiled Moe's
dad.
"Definitely!" Moe's mum nodded.
"Absolutely!" Even Maxwell agreed.

The last act, two hippos, walked out into the clearing.

"We're going to sing a yawning song," said one hippo.

"And you can join us. Sing along!" said the other hippo.

And the hippos started to yawn... and to YAWN... and to YAWN!! It was very strange music! It was music made up of tongues and tonsils and teeth! But before long, everyone in the audience was joining in — yawning and stretching and yawning some more.

Each group of animals began to wander off, calling "Goodnight!" to their friends. And as they went, they were still yawning.

"The hippos never fail. They're always the best act to end the show," smiled the lion beside Moe. Then he had a good yawn himself.

"Goodbye, Moe."

"You were wonderful."

"Next year, you must give us an even longer rhyme."

Lots of different animals came up to Moe and congratulated her before they went home.

Moe, Maxwell and Mr and Mrs Crocodile dived back into the watering hole and swam down to their home.

"I've got something I can do now," said Moe.

"What's that?" asked Moe's mum.

"I make up poems all the time.
I like it! It just suits me fine!" said Moe, happily.

"Yes dear. Well, off you go to bed," said Moe's mum.

"You can make up more rhymes in your sleep," said Moe's dad.

And that's just what Moe did!

Mug

On the banks of a river, deep in Africa, there
lived a crocodile. He was called Mug, which
was a fine name for a crocodile, and he liked
nothing more than to lie in the sun. Then,
when he felt a bit too hot, he would slither
into the river and swim down into the cool,
slimy depths.

Mug was a large crocodile. He had a long tail,
a hard, horny hide, and a great pair of jaws.
And in the jaws were his fine, curved teeth,
each one of them as sharp as any crocodile
could wish. All the animals round about were
frightened of Mug. And so would you be, if
you lived in a forest, because there was
always a chance that Mug would eat you.

Every morning, Mug would move slowly through the shallow water to the place where the animals liked to come for a drink. Only his eyes would show about the surface, and so it was hard for the animals to see where he was. But he was there all right, watching, waiting for his chance. Then, when an animal lowered its head to the water to drink, Mug would lurch forward and grab the poor creature by the nose.

"Oh dear," said the monkeys, as they watched safely from the trees above the river. "Mug's caught a warthog again."

Mug was frightened of nobody. There was no crocodile bigger than he, and certainly no other creature had teeth half as sharp as his. And so he just lay there and smiled to himself, thinking how lucky he was to be such a fine crocodile.

Now there's something you should know about crocodiles. They can't clean their teeth like people can – birds do it for them. As the crocodiles lie on the sandbanks with their jaws wide open, little white birds come and peck at the scraps of food in between the crocodiles' teeth. The birds get their meals that way, and it suits the crocodiles very well. Mug didn't like it. Whenever a bird tried to clean his teeth, he would bring his great jaws closed with a mighty snap, and the bird would fly away in a flurry of feathers. Sometimes Mug bit off a bird's tail, which made the monkeys laugh, but made all the other birds very cross.

"That Mug is just ungrateful," the birds said. "It'll serve him right if his teeth fall out." And that is just what happened. One day, while he was waiting to catch somebody at the river's edge, Mug felt something strange in his mouth.

He opened his jaws and wiggled them about a bit. But his mouth still felt odd, and when he next opened it, there plopped out into the river a large white tooth. Then, only a few minutes later, another one fell out, and another after that.

Mug felt very worried.

"What will happen to me if all my teeth fall out?" He asked himself. "How will I be able to pull my breakfast into the river by its nose?" He swam along feeling very miserable.

He didn't bother to swim underwater now, and so everybody was able to move away from the river bank well before he arrived. And by the time he got to the edge of the water, more teeth had fallen out. He now had no teeth at all, and his great jaws had nothing but soft pink gums in them.

Mug sank beneath the surface of the water and waited.

"I can still try to get my breakfast," he said. "Perhaps I'll be able to hold it with my gums."

He had some time to wait, but at last a young zebra came down to the edge of the water to drink. This zebra had been told by its parents to be very careful about water, because they knew all about Mug and his wicked ways, but the youngster had forgotten their advice. Now he stood with his nose in the water, while only inches away lay Mug, watching him with his sunken eyes.

Suddenly Mug shot forward, opening his jaws wide, and then, snap! He caught hold of the poor zebra's nose.

It was very sore having your nose pinched like that, but not as sore as if there had been teeth. The little zebra gave a snort and then, twisting his head to do so, gave Mug a hard bite on his crocodile nose. Mug let out a yell and shot back into the water.

"That hurt!" he cried out in anger. "You shouldn't bite people on the nose like that!" When they heard this, the monkeys in the trees almost fell out of their branches with laughter.

"Did you hear that?" they shouted gleefully.
"Mug says it's rude to bite other people's noses!
What has he been doing all the time, may we
ask?"

Mug looked up at the trees and opened his jaws
again to scare the monkeys, but of course they
weren't at all scared. All they saw was pink
gums, and pink gums can't do much harm, even
if they do belong to a great crocodile.

Poor Mug felt utterly ashamed. Slowly he swam away, to a part of the river where he could lie on the sand without being laughed at. He felt hungry too, as he had missed his breakfast. That zebra would have tasted very nice, he thought, but I'll never be able to catch anything again. I shall starve.

And he did. Slowly Mug became thinner and thinner. Nobody gave him any food, of course, because he had spent all his life biting people. If you bite people all your life, you end up with very few friends. In fact, you end up with none at all.

The monkeys watched Mug getting thinner
and weaker. After a few days, when he was so
weak that he could hardly even swim, they
began to feel sorry for him.

"He's not so bad," they said. "I suppose he
can't help being a crocodile."

So quietly and carefully they crept down out
of their trees. Mug was dozing on the sand
bank, dreaming of food. He didn't see the
monkeys, and what they brought him, and it
was only when he opened his eyes a little
while later that he saw what had happened.

There before him on the sand was a pile of bananas, all neatly laid out by the monkeys. Mug sniffed at them. He had never eaten bananas before. He had always called them "monkey food" and had laughed at them, but now that he was hungry, well, it was a little different.

"I might just take a little bite," Mug said to himself. "I'm sure that I won't like them, but there's no harm in trying."

Mug opened his great jaws, slowly, of course, since he was so weak. Then he closed them on a banana and began to chew. You don't need teeth to eat bananas, and for somebody who has nothing but gums they are ideal food.

"Mmm," said Mug. "That wasn't so bad after all." He ate another banana, and then another, and soon all the bananas were gone. This made him feel much better. He had guessed that the monkeys had brought them to him, and so he thought that he should go and say thank you. The monkeys were very pleased when Mug came to thank them, and they were even more pleased when he offered to carry them across the river on his back. There were many more banana trees on the other side, but they had never been able to get across the water.

Now they could collect more bananas than they would ever need, and they could give the extra ones to their new friend Mug.

Mug grew fat on bananas, but he didn't mind. Everybody liked him now that he had stopped biting people, and the monkeys were proud of the great fat crocodile who carried them across the river in such style.

Every so often, while the monkeys were riding on his back, Mug thought it might be nice to eat a monkey. But he never did, of course, because it is impossible to eat a monkey if you have no teeth. And also he remembered that it was rude to bite your friends, and even ruder to eat them. So he stuck to bananas, and everybody thought that this was just the right thing to do.

Jonathan

Upon the swampy slimy banks of the River Nile
Lived a great big family of crocodiles.
All day long they wrestled through the deep
Or rolled around the reeds, in a rocky, crocky
heap.

Each one strong with great clutching claws,
Needle-sharp teeth in giant snapping jaws.
Scaly green skin and darting black eyes,
Wading through the river under African skies.

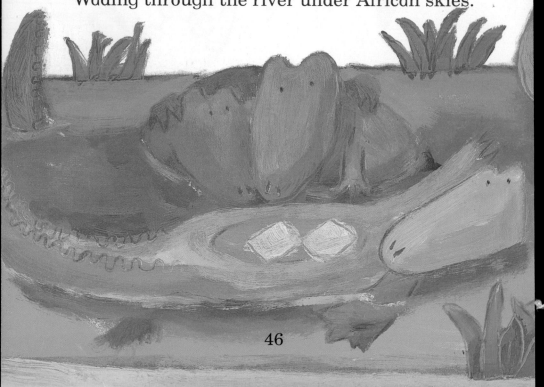

But, one in particular was quite different
from the others
Not a bit like his cousins or his sisters or his
brothers
He wasn't any weaker, or even any shorter,
But this strange croc was afraid of the water.

His name was Jonathan. Poor old Jonathan.

Now, as you can imagine, it was a terrible thing,
To be a great big crocodile who really couldn't
swim
The very thought of sliding into that deep and
muddy river
Was enough to leave poor Jonathan a-tremble
and a-quiver.

Jonathan. Poor old Jonathan.

His friends, encouraged him with inflatable
things
Like armbands, floats and rubber rings
They even threw him a knotted rope —
But nope — that rope only made him choke.

"You know," said his friends, "you really oughter
try putting ONE foot into that water —
It may well be that you'd feel better
If you got your toes just a weeny bit wetter."

But no. It was no use. No use at all.

For the closer he got, the more he'd flinch;
He couldn't step in, even half an inch.
No matter how many times he tried
Jonathan became more and more petrified.

Miserably he hid beneath his tail
And cried out loud in a shameful wail;
"How on earth will I learn to swim
When I'm far too scared to tip-toe in!"

Jonathan. Poor old Jonathan.

Well it drove his mother completely potty,
She told him off and smacked his botty,
She said, "It's time you stopped these silly fears
And wiped away those crocodile tears."

"OH! ... How I wish I had a daughter
Instead of a son who's afraid of the water
So hurry up and learn to swim —
Or else I'll jolly well PUSH you in!"

Jonathan. Poor old Jonathan.

But something curious happened one day
As Jonathan watched his friends at play;
Up the river a boat came steaming,
Packed with passengers, shouting and
screaming.

The foaming water seemed all too near
To those on board who trembled with fear
As the crocs could hardly wait a sec
To sniff the juicy bait on deck.

So in order to avoid the dangerous crocs
The driver swerved but hit the rocks.
He crashed the boat with such a whack
That a little girl slipped — and fell off the back.

"HELP! HELP!" She cried — "I'VE FALLEN IN!
I'M GOING TO DROWN — I CANNOT SWIM!
IF YOU DON'T FISH ME OUT OF THIS
CROCKY RIVER
THEY'LL MUNCH MY BONES AND SUCK
MY LIVER!"

Without a moment's pause for thinking
About slipping or sliding or drowning or
sinking,
Into the water Jonathan plunged
And towards that child he bravely lunged.

Two rows of teeth as sharp as scissors
Grabbed the girl by her frilly knickers,
Opening his jaws up tremendously wide
He tossed the screaming child inside.

Everyone stared as Jonathan caught her
Before she sank beneath the water
Cushioned upon his gooey tongue
He swiftly swam her back to mum.

Well! – The crocodiles gasped in shock and
surprise
They clapped and danced and dried their eyes
Even the hippos and rhinos joined in –
"IT'S JONATHAN! JONATHAN! HE'S
LEARNT TO SWIM!"

Jonathan! Good old Jonathan!

B U T! ... Just as Jonathan reached the boat
The little girl slipped — and fell down his
throat
She wriggled and squiggled and gave a shout
"IT SMELLS IN HERE — PLEASE LET ME
OUT!"

And without so much as a nibble or chew
He opened his mouth and out she flew!
The people yelled and cheered and roared
As the girl plopped safely back on board.

"THANK YOU!" she cried. "You saved my life!
If I weren't a human I'd become your wife!"
And leaning over the rickety deck
She kissed his lips and hugged his neck.

"Oh! Please! — Don't thank me more my dear;
It was YOU who saved ME from a terrible fear."
And bursting with joy and merrily grinning
He dived back down for a little more swimming!

Jonathan! Good old Jonathan!

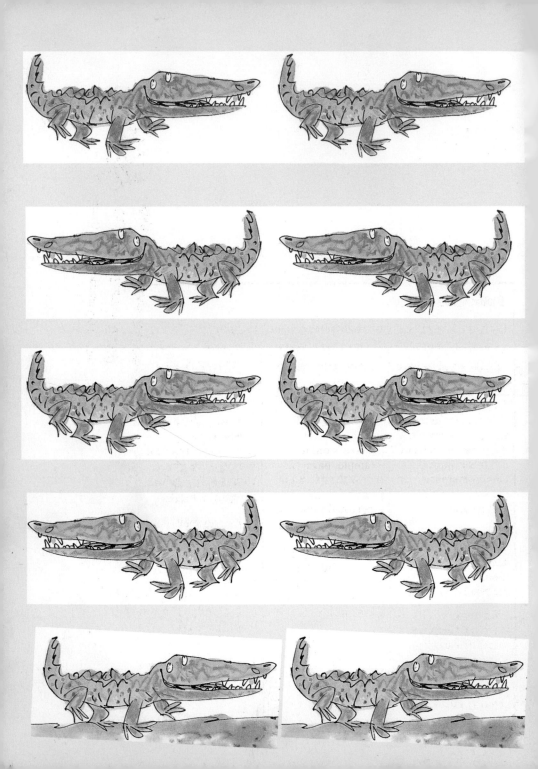